I'M FROM EVERYWHERE

Written by
Bird Collier

Dedicated to

King Collier & Our 3 Little Birds

Jamal stood at the door of his new classroom looking at all of the new faces.

"Hi, Come on in!" said Miss Thomas.

Jamal walked in and stood next to Ms. Thomas. He looked around the classroom. Jamal was in a new school, in a new city, and in a new state. He didn't know anyone.

"This is Jamal and he will be joining our class," Miss Thomas said to the class.

"We want to make Jamal feel welcome, so let's all give him a friendly hello."

"Hello!" The whole class said together. The sound of their hello was very loud and it made Jamal smile. Jamal counted fourteen classmates and picked out the kindest faces in the group. He was very good at that. Jamal had a lot of practice with meeting new people and making new friends.

"We already have a great desk picked out for you Jamal," said Miss Thomas. She pointed towards an empty desk. Jamal looked over and saw that his new desk was close to the window. He would be able to look out at the clouds and birds sometimes. Jamal was happy about his new desk.

"Before you take your seat, will you tell us where you are from so that we can place a pin on our class map?" asked Miss Thomas.

Jamal looked over at the map Miss Thomas was pointing to. The map was hanging on the wall. There were fourteen bright red push pins on the map. Most of the pins were very close together inside of Texas. A few of the pins were a little further away, but not too far. Miss Thomas held out a box of red capped push pins so Jamal could take one.

Jamal cleared his throat. "Well, I'm from everywhere Miss Thomas," Jamal said.

The class laughed. Miss Thomas' eye brows went up high, with surprise.

"Really?" she asked. "EVERYWHERE?"

Jamal shrugged his shoulders. "Well yes, kind of," he replied.

"Okay, tell us more about that Jamal," Miss Thomas said with a smile.

Jamal took the box of pins and walked towards the map.

"Both of my parents are in the military so I have lived in a lot of different places,"

he explained. "I was born in Spain. In Spain I learned lots of Spanish words like *Hola* and *Adios* which mean hello and goodbye. My favorite Spanish food was *Paella*." Jamal placed a pin in the map on Spain.

"After Spain we were stationed in Hawaii. Hawaii was beautiful and I could go to the beach almost every day!" Jamal exclaimed.

"Cool!" whispered some of Jamal's classmates. Jamal placed a pin in the biggest Hawaiian island. "I learned some Hawaiian words like *Aloha* which means both hello and goodbye. I even learned to say *Mele Kaliki Maka*, which means Merry Christmas. At home I have a collection of lava rocks from the Volcano on Oahu."

"I loved Hawaii, but I really liked our next station too! After Hawaii, we were transferred to Panama. In Panama they spoke Spanish just like in Spain. It was nice to be able to practice my Spanish because I had forgotten some of it. In Panama, my friends taught me to play soccer. Sometimes we would play soccer until it was dark and our mothers made us come inside. I also learned a lot about the wildlife in Panama. Sometimes there were monkeys, sloths, and snakes right in our backyard. "Whoa!" one of the kids on the front row said. Jamal smiled and kept talking. "The monkeys stayed high in the trees and never came down to bother us, but they were so much fun to watch." Jamal pushed a pin into Panama on the map.

South Carolina

Shrimp Grits

"After Panama, my dad was sent overseas on a deployment. A deployment is when someone in the military has to go work in a place where they are not allowed to take their family. That was hard because I missed my dad so much.

While dad was away on his deployment, my brother, sister, mom and I lived in South Carolina close to family. Living in South Carolina was the first time I had ever lived in a place where I could see my grandparents, cousins, aunts and uncles any time I wanted to. Being with other family was fun and helped make it easier to wait for my dad to come home from deployment. We had family cookouts, birthday parties, and even a family reunion. At night all of us would catch lightning bugs in a jar. It was like having a flashlight made of bugs." The class laughed excitedly and Jamal pushed a pin into South Carolina.

"After my dad came home, we lived in New Mexico. It was hot and dry there like a desert. During the summer the heat would be more than 100 degrees almost every day. At our house in New Mexico we had rocks and a prickly cactus in our yard instead of grass because the weather makes it hard to keep grass alive."

Jamal pushed his last pin into New Mexico and walked back to Miss Thomas.

"Those are some pretty incredible experiences, Jamal!" Miss Thomas exclaimed.

"But it must have been difficult for you to move around so much. Is it hard to start over in a new place?" she asked. Jamal thought about the question Miss Thomas had asked a little before he answered her.

"In all of the places I have lived, I have made some friends that were hard to leave behind. But my parents taught us that we were always just saying see you later, and never goodbye. Sometimes when we move to a new place, we find out that friends from our old school were transferred to the new place also. But, even if they were not transferred with us, we still try to stay in touch with them. I have learned to make new friends wherever I go. Now I have friends all over the world that I can visit.

"Wow, Jamal! That is wonderful," said Miss Thomas. "Thank you for sharing such exciting information with the class. Class, let's all thank Jamal for sharing."

The class clapped. Jamal walked to his seat and looked at his shiny red pins on the map. Five pins just for him, all spread out. Jamal was happy about his pins.

He had a good feeling about this new school and about the 14 new faces.

Epilogue

Little Jamal is a part of a military family. That means that one or more of his parents serves or has served in the military. In the United States there are five different branches of the military: Air Force, Army, Marines, Navy and Coast Guard. Each branch does its part to keep our country safe and protect the pursuit of freedom all over the world.

Even though Jamal is not in the military himself, everyone in a military family has a role in helping the service member be successful. Sometimes that means moving every few years and having to leave friends behind. Sometimes that also means living without a parent who is deployed overseas. These sacrifices can be hard. But, these sacrifices also help children of military families develop skills that not everyone has. For example, Jamal is good at meeting new people and he can tell a lot about a person just by reading their faces. Jamal has also learned how to stay in touch with friends that he does not get to see. Long distance friends are not always easy to keep up with. Jamal is very good at hellos and goodbyes. He knows how to see the bright side of any new situation and how to enjoy change. Jamal has also seen a lot of the world. All of his traveling has helped him learn about different languages and cultures. Military families are a very special part of American culture.

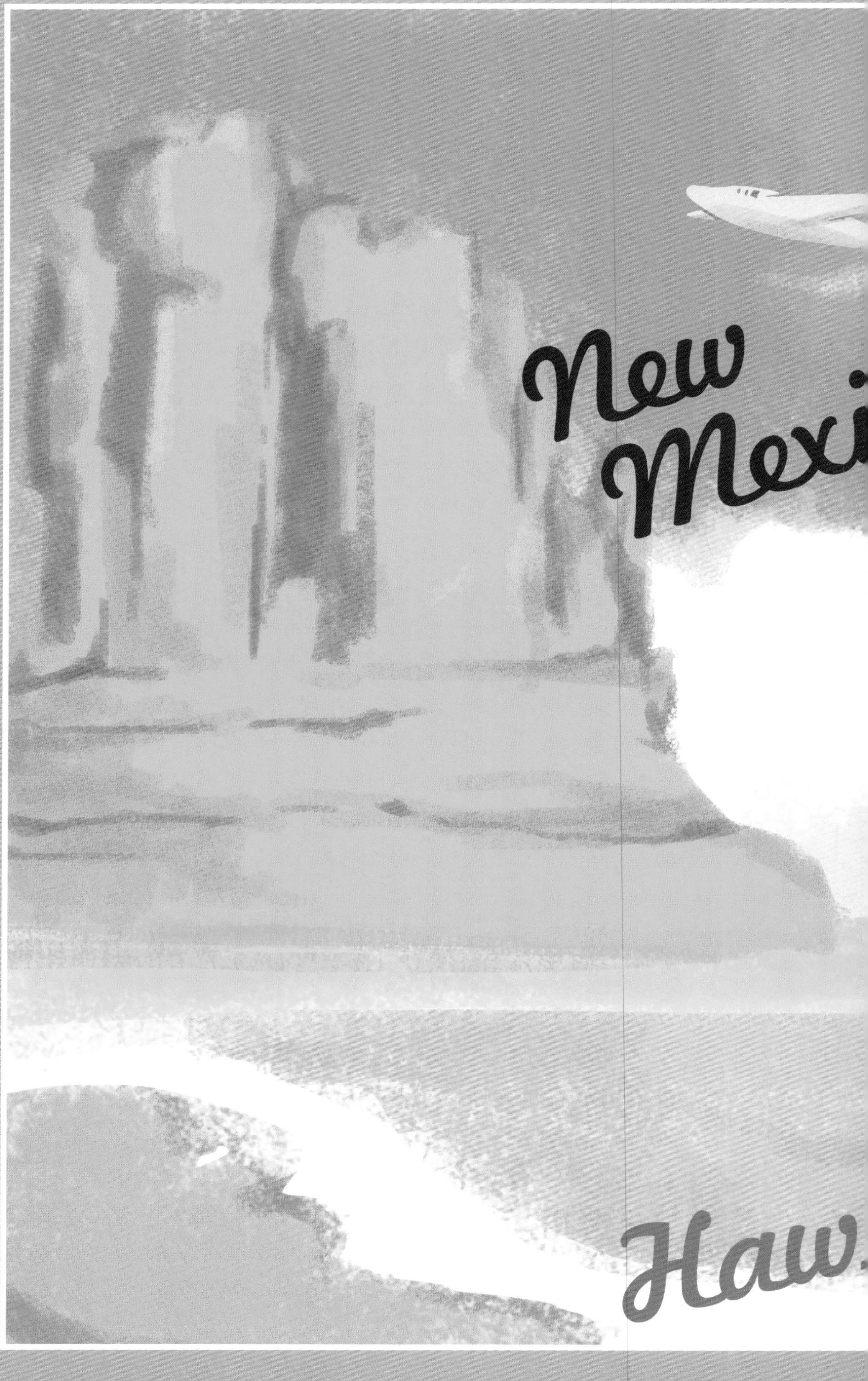
New
Mexi
Haw